To Gregg, for your
unending support.

www.mascotbooks.com

The Big Bad WHAAAAT????

©2018 Eileen R. Malora. All Rights Reserved. No part of this publication
may be reproduced, stored in a retrieval system or transmitted in any
form by any means electronic, mechanical, or photocopying, recording or
otherwise without the permission of the author.

For more information, please contact:
Mascot Books
620 Herndon Parkway #320
Herndon, VA 20170
info@mascotbooks.com

Library of Congress Control Number: 2017908975

CPSIA Code: PRT1017A
ISBN-13: 978-1-68401-360-9

Printed in the United States

The Big Bad
WHAAAAT?????

Written by Eileen R. Malora

Illustrated by Alycia Pace

Everyone thinks they know the story of a little
girl with a red cape and basket of baked goods.
But this is *my* side, kept quiet by the people
around the neighborhoods.

I am a retired police dog and Jax is my name.
To serve and protect was the name of the game.

One day while out walking my beat,
the little girl in question crossed the street.

Into the woods she went without fear.
My instincts were to protect, so I stayed near.

The little girl stopped, turned slowly, and looked right at me.
I said "I'm Jax! I'll make sure you get where you are going safely!"

She was startled, and began to talk quick:
"I'm bringing baked goods to my grandma, she's sick!"

I replied, "I'm sorry your grandmother is feeling so blue.
Why don't you pick some flowers and bring them to her too?"

I *sprinted* ahead to make sure everything was safe and secure.
When I got there, I knocked on the door.

Her grandmother had just finished making some chicken soup.
She saw me tired, thirsty, and hungry sitting on her stoop.

She was kind, felt sorry for me, and invited me in.
She gave me a pillow, some water, and a piece of chicken.

Boy was I hungry, because I swallowed it whole.
Before I knew it, I was choking as my head hit the bowl.

Grandma jumped right into action and opened my mouth.
Reached in to find the bone that was heading south.

Farther and farther she went into my throat!
I hiccupped! Swallowed Grandma and began to bloat!!!

Oh dear! OH MY! What am I going to do??
Knowing the little girl would be here in just a few.

Panicked, I put on Grandma's clothes and jumped in her bed.
I heard a **knock** on the door and wished Grandma had swallowed me instead.

I knew what had to be done so I wouldn't scare the child.

But I started feeling sick. My stomach going **wild!**

I would pretend to be Grandma when she came to my side.
What else could I do? The little girl would have cried.

She began, "What **big** eyes you have grandma! They're so pretty."
I replied, "Thank you my dear," my heart swelling with pity.
"What big ears you have!" the little girl said.
My stomach was grumbling. I wanted **out** of that bed!

I was going to be sick, that was for sure!
I let out a **BURP** so **BIG** it blew open the door.

The little girl shouted, "Wow! Grandma that really smells *foul!*"
My head was spinning, sweat was dripping,
and I let out a **GROWL**.

The **gurgling**, the **grumbling**, "**NEVER AGAIN!**" I swore!
With another huge **BELCH**, Grandma popped out onto the floor.

The two were so happy, they hugged and realized now it all made sense.

I shouted, **"I was only trying to help!"** That was my defense.

So now you know the story of the little girl
and her grandma, completely updated.

We can finally put to rest the version that has
been greatly exaggerated.

No one really understood what happened to me.
So I'm moving on to a neighboring city.

I've decided to become a different kind of protector.
I saw an ad for a job as a building inspector.

To Be Continued…

About the Author

Eileen lives in Rockland County, New York with her husband Gregg and three children. They own two rescue dogs—a pitbull named Cooper, from Hi-Tor Animal Shelter, and a rat terrier named Ottis. This is Eileen's first book.

Have a book idea?

Contact us at:

info@mascotbooks.com | www.mascotbooks.com